100
Sex Positions

The erotic handbook with 100 sex positions
to try out and discover.
Each position with graphic and explanation.
For more fun in everyday life.

Meaning of
the symbols:

Anal suitable

Sporty

Quick & easy

Y-CURVE - POSITION

The „Y-Curve" is not an expression of mathematics, but means a lot of fun! Here's how it works: she lies flat on her stomach on the bed and slides her upper body over the edge of the bed. So far that she's hanging off the bed by the waist. She supports herself with her hands on the floor and opens her legs a little. He penetrates her from behind - with his stretched legs between hers. He holds on to her bottom and stretches out his upper body so that a „Y" is formed.

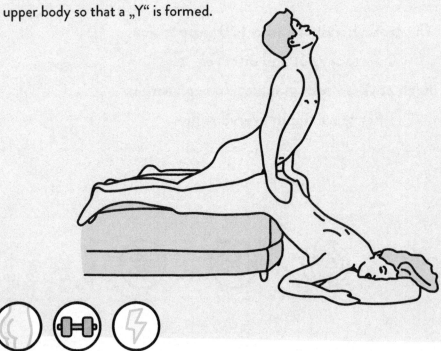

4

FRANKA BURGMULLER

100 Sex Positions

THE EROTIC HANDBOOK

LOOTY

THE PINWHEEL - POSITION

Things get hot in the „Firewheel" position. This is how it works: Both sit opposite each other on the bed. She wraps her legs around his waist so that her pelvis rests on his lap and supports herself with her arms behind her. He shifts his weight onto one elbow, twisting his body slightly to one side. He wraps his legs around her waist. Now he can penetrate her by inserting his penis inside her with his free hand.

INDRANI - POSITION

More depth, more stimulation? Then the „Indrani" position is just right for you. She lies relaxed on her back and bends her legs towards her breasts. He kneels in front of her, weight shifted forward, and penetrates her. This position is also particularly good for anal sex.

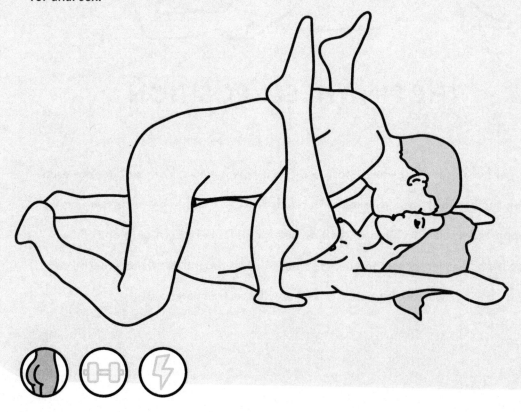

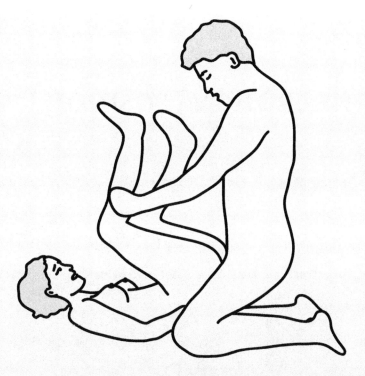

BOUNCY HERO - POSITION

The position „Bouncy Hero" is good for a particularly strong G-spot stimulation. Here's how it works: The woman lies comfortably on her back, drawing her legs, stretched out, to her chest. He kneels in front of her and penetrates her. With one hand he supports himself on the floor and with the other on the inner thigh, from her.

THE EROTIC V - POSITION

Do you need a challenging position? Then have fun with the „Erotic V" position. She sits on the edge of a table or countertop. He stands in front of her with slightly bent knees. She grabs his neck and pulls one leg up over his shoulder, then the other on the other side. Your legs are stretched. He supports her hold by holding her bottom. Made? Well then, let's get down to business...

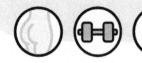

THE PADLOCK - POSITION

Another creative way to have sex is „The Padlock". This position goes like this: She sits on a slightly higher surface (e.g. a countertop, table or washing machine) and leans back on her hands. He stands in front of her and penetrates her while she closes her legs tightly around his waist. He sets the intensity with his thrusts.

ARMISTICE - POSITION

The "Armistice" position is not only suitable for make-up sex. He stretches out on his side. She lies on her back at right angles to him, with her legs across his waist. A comfortable position that leaves your hands free for tenderness.

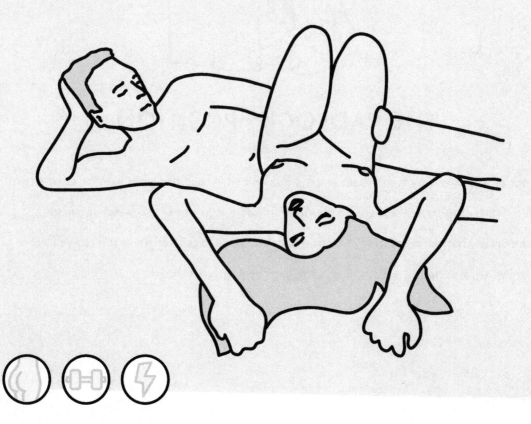

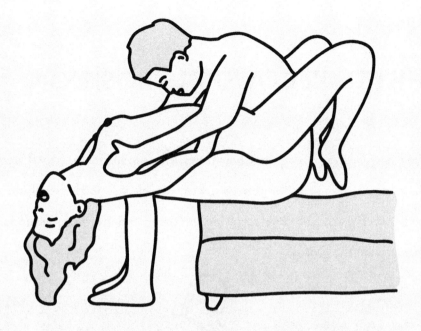

UPSIDE DOWN - POSITION

Build the „Upside Down" position into your sweetheart hour. The position works like this: He sits on a chair or the edge of the bed. She sits on his lap and wraps her legs around his waist. After that, she leans back completely and holds on to him. He either enjoys the view or buries his head in her breasts. Some sportiness is required here.

THE CHAIR COWGIRL - POSITION

Would you like a new position? Try „The Chair Cowgirl" position. This is how it works: You need a chair, stool, exercise ball or something similar. He sits on the stool, she sits on his lap with her legs apart. She can determine the speed and intensity by supporting herself with her toes on the ground.

THE CHALLENGE - POSITION

„The Challenge" position is not that big of a challenge. She stands on a chair and crouches slightly. The upper body is bent forward and the elbows are supported on the knees. He stands behind her and holds her waist. Now he can control the strokes and rhythm. You should be a little flexible.

13

SUPER-G - POSITION

Whatever you do today, don't forget the „Super-G" position. Here's how it works: The man kneels behind her and grabs her hips while she enjoys the game on all fours, head down. Either he sets the pace or she - with a thrusting movement.

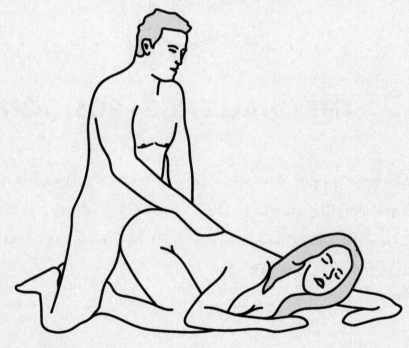

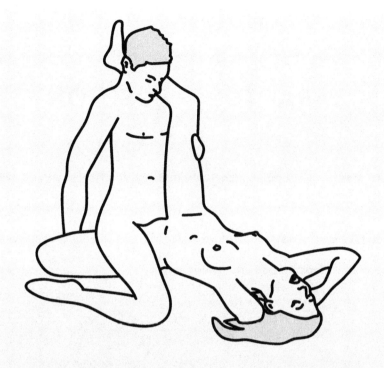

LEG EXTENSION - POSITION

Time for a new position?! The „Leg Extension" position works like this: She lies relaxed on her back. He kneels in front of her. She then puts her leg on his shoulder and he penetrates her. Deep penetration is guaranteed here and therefore a lot of fun.

TARANTULA - POSITION

The „Tarantula" position is popular with many men. Here's how she goes: He sits on the floor with his legs stretched out and shifts his weight back onto his hands. She sits on his lap and lets his penis penetrate. Then she also shifts her weight backwards onto her hands. She can now control speed and intensity.

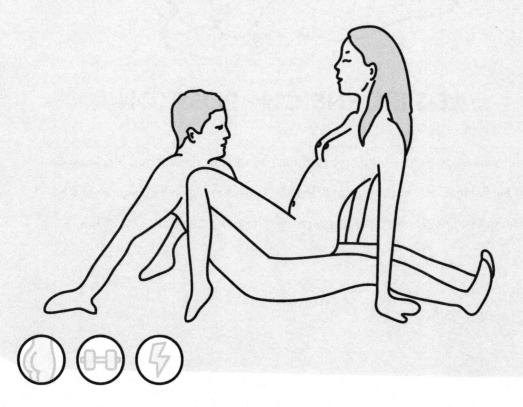

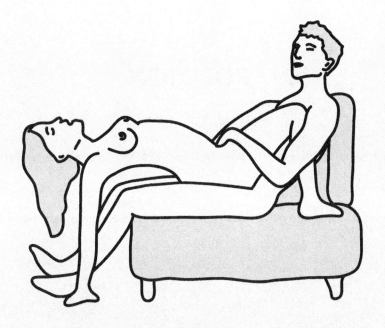

BED CAREER - POSITION

Would you like a new position? Here comes the „Bed Career" position and it goes like this: The man sits on an armchair or a couch with an armrest. Feet touch the floor, back leaning against it. She climbs forward onto his lap and lets her torso fall back. So far that she can support herself with her hands on the ground. She can set the pace by opening and closing her thighs.

69 - POSITION

A very well-known and popular position is the infamous "69". An absolute classic that you should definitely try. Lie on top of each other upside down and spoil each other. Use all your senses to bring the other into ecstasy and to receive ecstasy from the other.

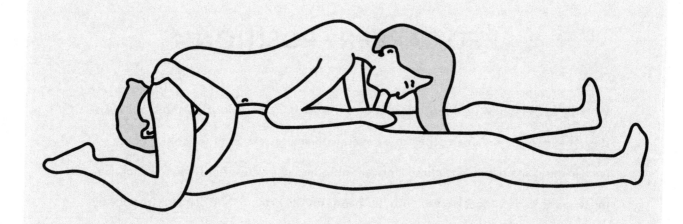

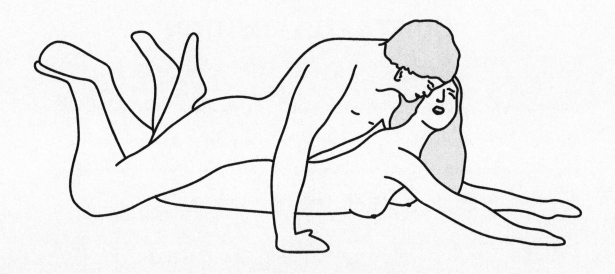

ELEPHANT - POSITION

An animal position is the „Elephant" position: She lies on her stomach and makes herself comfortable, her legs slightly apart. The man lays on her from behind and supports himself with his hands as if he were doing push-ups. Now he can slowly penetrate her while she can control the thrusts with gentle movements, back and forth.

QUIET BALL - POSITION

The "Quiet Ball" position is anything but quiet. This is how it works: The man sits on the bed with his legs slightly bent. She sits on his lap with her back towards him. He gently penetrates her. Now she bends forward, puts her hands on his feet and rocks up and down. Warning: you should be a bit flexible for this position.

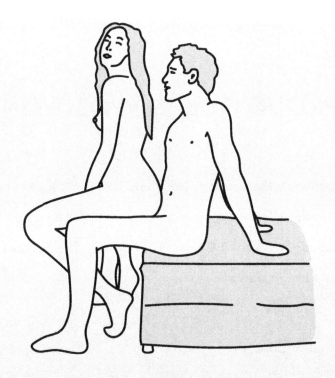

THE GOAT AND THE TREE - POSITION

This pose, whimsically named „The Goat And The Tree" goes like this: He sits on the edge of the bed, a chair, or something similar, and lets himself fall back onto his arms. She then sits on his lap with her back to him and leans forward slightly. Now she supports herself with her hands on his knees and sets the pace and intensity.

PROUD QUEEN - POSITION

An almost royal position is the position „The Proud Queen". It works like this: the man lies relaxed on his back while the woman gracefully sits on his hips, buttocks to his face. The woman can support herself with her hands on his legs. The man can now enjoy the view and watch his adorable queen in ecstasy.

22

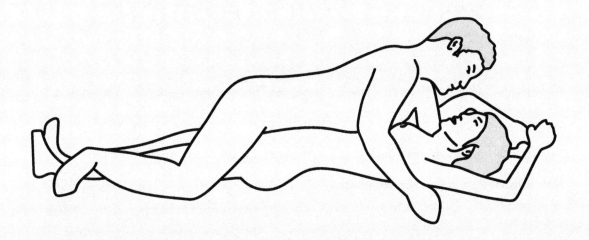

THE NIRVANA - POSITION

The position „Nirvana" promises a lot of fun and it works like this: The woman lies
on her back, stretches her legs and arms. He lies down on her. While he's inside her,
she tenses all her muscles and pulls her thighs together to build tension. The woman
can reinforce the effect by supporting herself on the upper and lower bed frame. This
intensifies the penetration effect and thus the fun.

PARVATI'S DANCE - POSITION

A pose to enjoy is the „Parvati's Dance" position. This is how it works: He lies relaxed on his back. She sits towards him on his lap. She presses his penis tightly with her thighs. She supports herself backwards with her arms and can control the experience with sensual up and down movements.

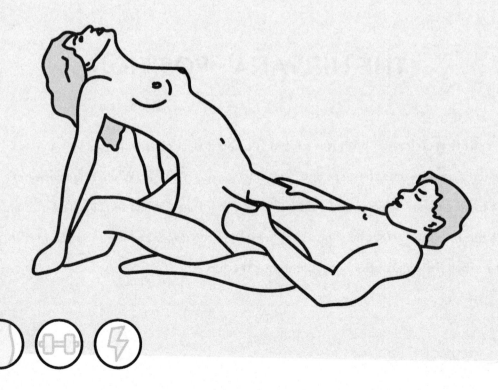

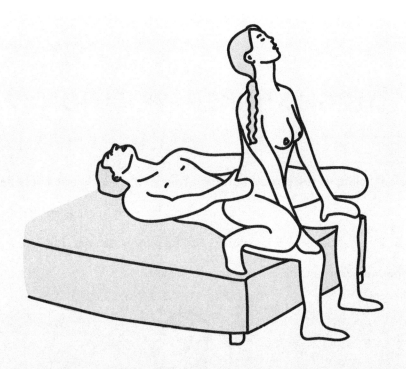

THE ENJOYER - POSITION

She gets her money's worth in the „Enjoyer" position. He sits on the edge of a bed or an armchair. She sits down on his lap with her back to him. She places her feet on his right and left so that he can penetrate her deeply. The more stable the ground, the easier.

THIGH STRIKER - POSITION

The mountain is calling in the position „Thigh Striker". It works like this: He lies relaxed on his back and bends his legs. She sits down on his lap with her legs spread and her bottom towards him. She leans on his knees and he penetrates her. He enjoys a sexy view while she rides the penis.

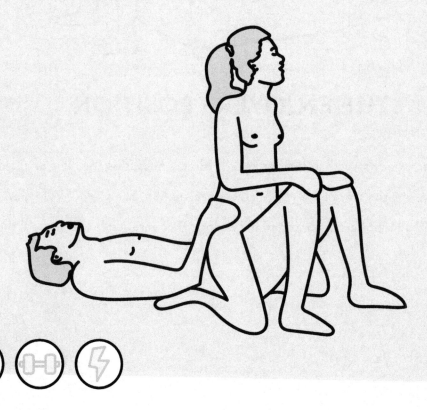

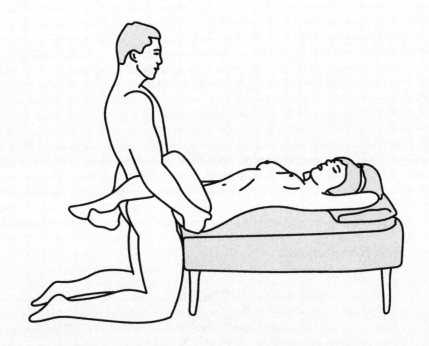

RELAXED GIRL - POSITION

This is for all late risers - the „Relaxed Girl" position. It works like this: She lies comfortably in bed with her legs up and her head resting gently on a pillow. He kneels in front of her, holding her waist. She opens her thighs and he can penetrate her.

SIDEKICK - POSITION

The right kick at the right moment, the „Sidekick" position works like this: She lies slightly sideways on the bed, with her back up. One leg is stretched, the other slightly bent. He kneels behind her and slides a knee between her legs and penetrates her. The deep penetration guarantees fun.

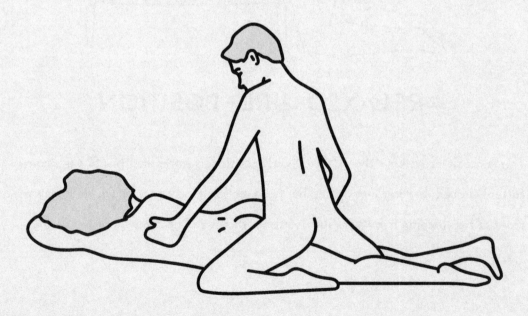

BRIDGE PIER - POSITION

A new position in your collection: the „Bridge Pier" position (Caution: things are really sporty here!). He sits down on a solid surface with his legs bent and supports himself with his hands behind him. Now he pushes his hips up in the air in the form of a bridge. She sits on top of his stiff penis and sets the depth and rhythm.

29

DECKCHAIR - POSITION

It doesn't just sound comfortable, it is! The „Deckchair" position. Here's how it works:
He lies down on the bed with his legs stretched out and leaning back on his hands. She
lies down comfortably with her head on a pillow in front of him and rests her legs on his
shoulders. He can penetrate deep into her and that makes for an intense experience.

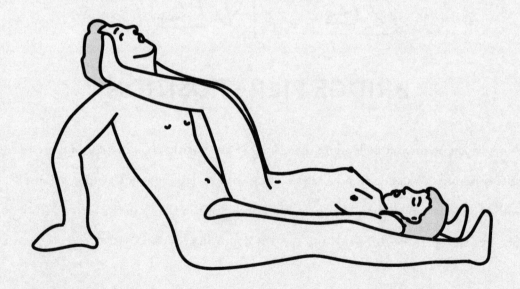

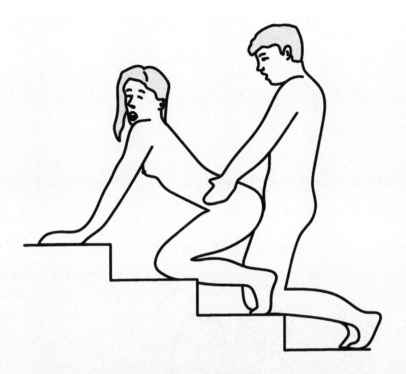

STAIRCASE AFFAIR - POSITION

A pose that can also be practiced outside is the "Staircase Affair" position. All you need is a staircase. She kneels on a step and leans forward. She supports herself with her hands on the upper steps of the stairs. He kneels behind her, also on the steps, grabs her waist and penetrates her.

STANDING - POSITION

The „Standing" position is particularly practical for many places with little space, such as the airplane toilet or changing room. Just face each other, she presses her pelvis against him and her upper body slightly backwards, and you're good to go. You should be about the same size, otherwise a small increase can compensate for the difference in size.

SENSUAL CRISS-CROSS - POSITION

Try the „Sensual Criss-Cross" position, it works like this: She lies comfortably on her side and lifts her top leg. He lies down and slips between them at right angles. Now he penetrates her and can put his hands on her shoulders for more stability.

RIGHT ANGLE - POSITION

Try the „Right Angle" position. It's very simple and goes like this: Lie flat on your back on a table with your bottom on the edge of the table. She bends her legs slightly. He stands on the edge in front and penetrates her. A pillow is helpful so that he can reach the right height.

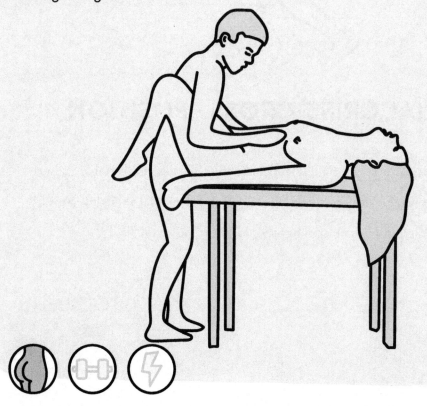

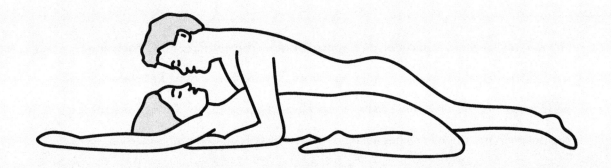

SEDUCTION DANCE - POSITION

A hot position is the „Seduction Dance" position. Here's how: She kneels on the bed and slowly lets herself fall backwards until she's lying on her back, but her legs are still bent. She stretches her arms up as he lays on top of her and penetrates her.

35

THE VIRGIN - POSITION

The "Virgin" position is particularly intense for him. She lies flat on her back and squeezes her thighs together. Similar to the missionary position, he lies over her. Only his legs are left and right, next to her closed legs. He penetrates through the narrow gap between her thighs and has a particularly intense feeling during sex. Also works great the other way around, so he below and she above (as in the picture).

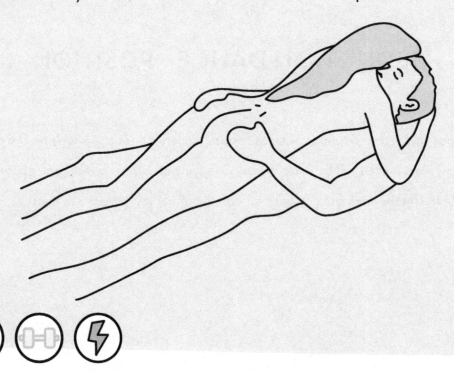

MILK AND WATER - POSITION

The „Milk and Water" position is a little more exotic. This is how it works: He sits at the head of the bed with his legs stretched out. She sits sideways on his lap and puts an arm around his shoulders. He keeps pulling her towards him, causing her to move up and down. Hot kisses and looks included.

BIG DIPPER - POSITION

Try the „Big Dipper" position today. It works like this: She lies on her stomach on the bed, so far down that her legs dangle down. He stands at the edge of the bed between her legs and pulls them up to him. She braces herself on her elbows as he penetrates her. She stands in the air like a wheelbarrow.

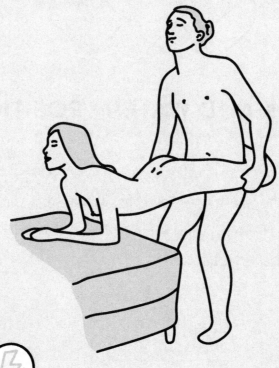

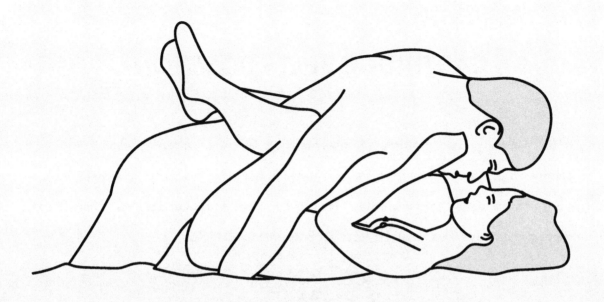

FACE-TO-FACE - POSITION

The „Face-To-Face" position is intense and romantic. How it works: Both lie on their side or she on her back, with their faces turned to each other. She gently wraps her legs around his waist. While he penetrates her, she can caress his balls with her hands and exchange deep looks with him.

CARTRIDGE BELT - POSITION

In the „Cartridge Belt" position, the shots are fired. This is how it works: She lies comfortably on her back, spreads her legs and pulls her legs towards her. He kneels in front of her and pulls her towards him. He lifts her pelvis and penetrates her. While she supports her feet on his chest, he rests her bottom on his thighs.

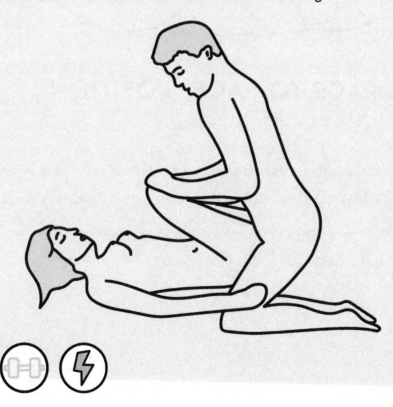

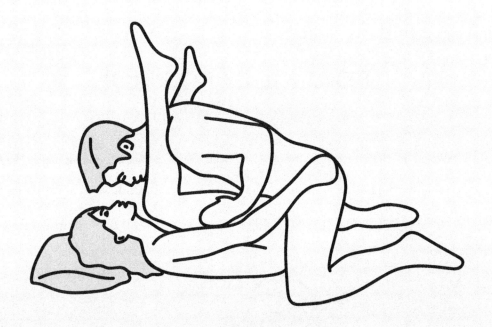

SNAIL - POSITION

The „Snail" position offers a particularly intense angle and high level of stimulation.

She lies down on the bed and pulls her legs to her breasts. He sits in front of her so that

she can rest her feet on his shoulders. Now he bends over her and penetrates her.

BOAT RIDE - POSITION

Ahoy! Would you like a new position? The „Boat Ride" position goes like this: He lies comfortably on the bed or another surface. She sits on him sideways, with her legs slightly apart, determining the depth and pace. Also great for outdoors, e.g. on the picnic blanket.

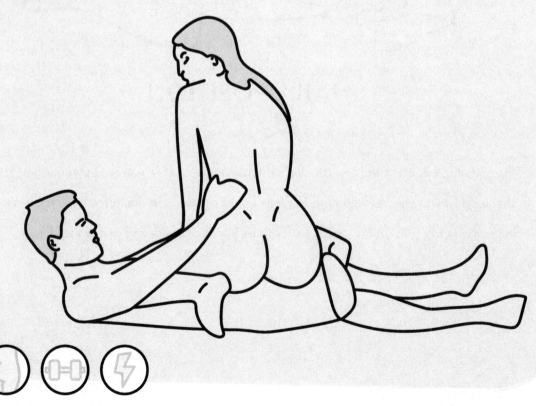

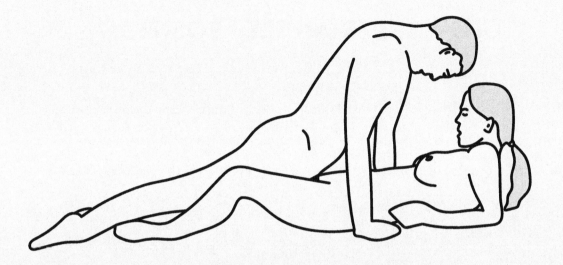

MISSIONARY - POSITION

The classic among the positions: the „Missionary" position. It simply belongs in a good collection! She is lying on the bed and he is facing her between her legs. You can stare deep into each other's eyes as he sets the pace and intensity of the sex. Too boring? Then get out of bed and find a more exciting place to do it.

43

GLOWING TRIANGLE - POSITION

Try the „Glowing Triangle" position. Basically, it works similar to the missionary position: She is lying on the bed and he is lying over her, but he is on all fours and she has to stretch her pelvis up in order for the sex to work. He stays in this position while she moves her pelvis up and down.

SCISSORS - POSITION

It's snap-snap in the „Scissors" position. This is how it works: She lies down on a table, e.g. garden table, coffee table or kitchen table. Her bottom is on the edge of the table, her legs are pointing upwards. He stands in front of her, grabs her legs by the ankles, opens her thighs and penetrates her. During sex, he repeatedly moves her legs together and opens them again.

THE MONKEY - POSITION

The „Monkey" position is animal good. It works like this: He lies on his back on the bed and pulls his legs up. She sits backwards with her bottom on his penis. She can lean on his feet and clasp his hands tightly for more support.

LOTUS - POSITION

Lovemaking the Asian way: the „Lotus" position. The position works as follows: He sits cross-legged, on the bed or on a carpet. She sits on his lap, facing him, and wraps her hands around his neck. She can either snuggle up to him or leave her legs stretched out.

BEGUILING BUTTERFLY - POSITION

A spring-like position is the „Beguiling Butterfly". She lies down with her bottom on the edge of a flat table, a coffee table for example. He stands in front of her and grabs her butt, lifting it up and penetrating her. Her legs are placed on his shoulders. She holds on to the edge of the table with her hands.

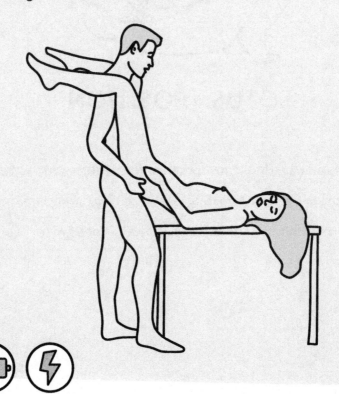

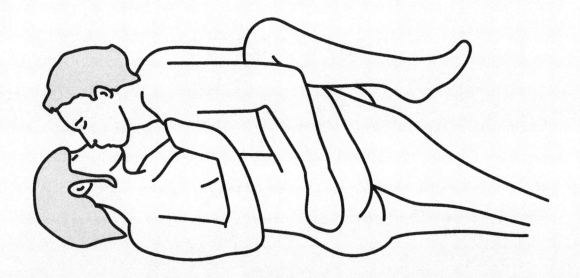

ZEN PAUSE - POSITION

The „Zen Pause" position works relaxed and with a lot of tenderness. Here's how it works: both lie on their sides so that they can look deep into each other's eyes. She swings a leg over his hips as he penetrates her. Tightly embraced and with gentle movements on the way to orgasm.

SPHINX - POSITION

Like the gods in Egypt, try the „Sphinx" position. This is how this graceful position works: She lies on her stomach and supports herself with her forearms in front. One of her legs is bent. He bends over her from behind and also supports himself with his hands. She arches her back a bit so he can penetrate her. Also very suitable for anal sex.

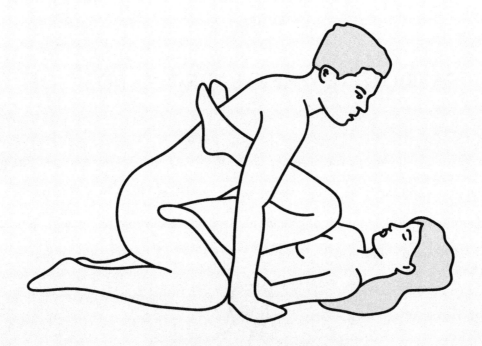

JELLY - POSITION

A low calorie dessert is the „Jelly" position. This is how it works: He kneels on the bed or on a soft surface. She lies on her back in front of him and sits with her buttocks on his lap. She opens her legs so he can penetrate. He can shift his weight slightly forward, onto his knees, while controlling the speed and intensity.

PASSIONATE WHEELBARROW - POSITION

This position is something for advanced users: the „Passionate Wheelbarrow". She gets on her knees and shifts her weight all the way forward onto her elbows. He stands behind her and grabs her ankles. She keeps her legs bent while he lifts her legs up to the wheelbarrow and penetrates her.

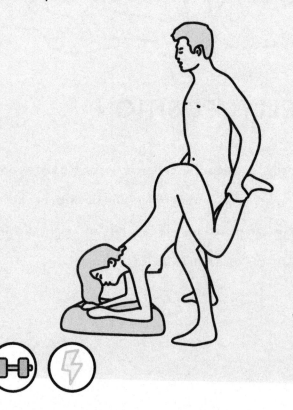

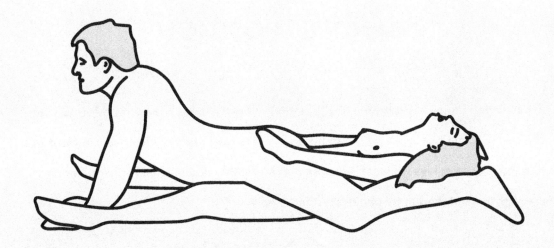

PROPELLER OF PASSION - POSITION

A position for sporty people, the „Propeller Of Passion". This is how it works: She lies comfortably on her back. He lays on her and penetrates her. Now he turns his hands and feet 360° on her like a propeller without slipping out of her. Definitely a fun position that can cause a laugh or two.

CANDLE - POSITION

A particularly intense position is the „Candle". How it works: She lies comfortably on the bed with her head on a pillow and pulls her legs towards her. He kneels in front of her and grabs her legs while penetrating her. Her pelvis is slightly raised and her legs are slightly stretched as he penetrates her deeply.

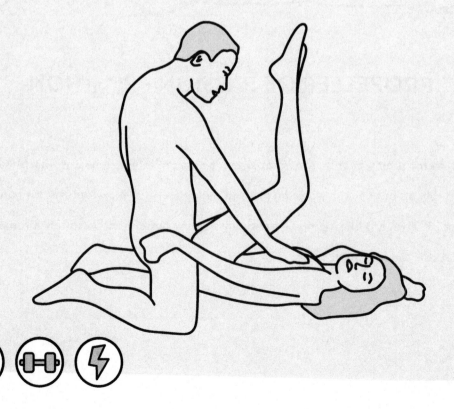

SEE-SAW - POSITION

Always on the move with the „See-Saw". This position goes like this: He lies down on a stable surface, e.g. on a carpet on the floor. One of his legs is stretched out while the other is slightly bent. She sits on his lap and clings to him. He holds her bottom for better support.

LEAPFROG - POSITION

Hop hop, the next one is the „Leapfrog" position and it goes like this: She kneels on the bed and leans her upper body all the way forward on her legs. He kneels behind her, leaning towards her with his knees on either side of her. Then he penetrates her and leans forward slightly.

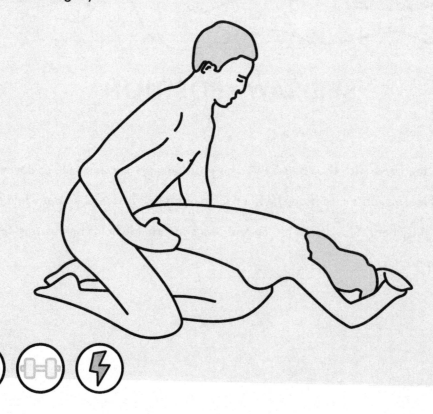

COWGIRL - POSITION

Another classic is the "Cowgirl" position. Be a cowboy and cowgirl and attach particular importance to a ride in the horse position. He makes himself comfortable lying down and she sits on his penis. She has the reins in her hand. Whether a sensual trot or a hard canter is entirely up to her. If you're bored, go out and go for a „horseback ride". In the long grass it will definitely give you that extra kick.

MERMAID - POSITION

Time for something new, the „Mermaid" position. This is how it works: She lies down on a table or the kitchen worktop. She stretches her legs straight up, closed. He stands in front of her on the edge and penetrates her. She can hold on to the edge. A little tip: a pillow under her butt can provide elevation for easier lovemaking.

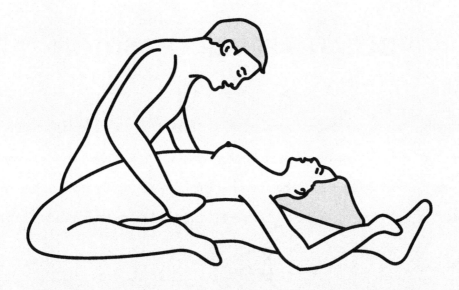

ARCH OF TRIUMPH - POSITION

Like the famous landmark of the city of love „The Arc De Triomphe". This is how it works: He lies down on the bed with his legs stretched out. She kneels on his lap so he can penetrate her. Now she leans back in the shape of an arch. He leans forward to her. Now the fun can begin. Vive la France!

VOLCANO FEVER - POSITION

Let it simmer with the „Volcano Fever" position. This is how she walks: She stands up, leans forward and supports herself with her hands on the bed, a table or, for the sporty, on the floor. Standing behind her, he grabs her thighs and pulls her towards him so her legs leave the floor. She tucks her legs under his arms and he penetrates her.

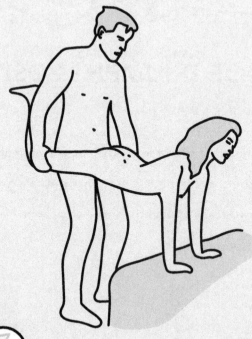

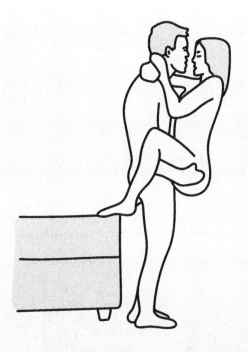

ASCENT TO LUST - POSITION

Do you already know the position „Ascent To Lust"? Try it out: It stands firmly on a solid surface. She stands in front of him and wraps her hands around his neck. He lifts her onto his hips and penetrates her while she supports herself with her feet on e.g. the bed. The ups and downs can become a sporting challenge.

LIMBO LOVE - POSITION

Try the „Limbo Love" position. This is how it works: He sits on an armchair or chair and uses a cushion to ensure that his legs are slightly elevated. She sits on his penis and throws her legs over his shoulders. He supports her with his hands and thighs so that she can lean back a little. Her hands are around his neck.

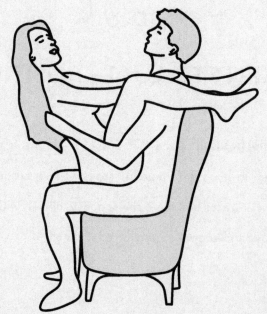

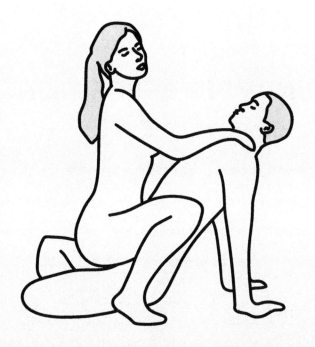

FANTASTIC ROCKING HORSE - POSITION

Yihaa, would you like a ride on the position: „The Fantastic Rocking Horse"? How it

works: He sits cross-legged and leans back on his hands. She sits on his lap, facing him.

She presses her thighs sideways against him. The rocking can begin.

NUMBER 8 - POSITION

The 8th day of the month is exactly the right day to try out the „Number 8". This is how it works: She lies down on the bed or a blanket in the countryside with her legs slightly raised. He lies across her, arms straight, like a push-up. She holds him by his waist as he penetrates her. Now he moves, in the form of an 8, in circular movements.

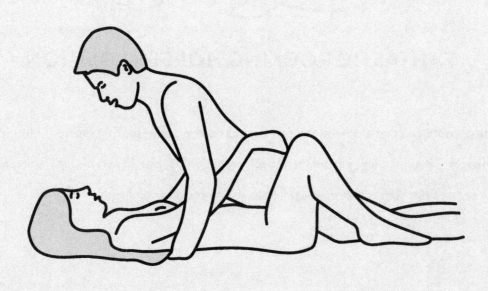

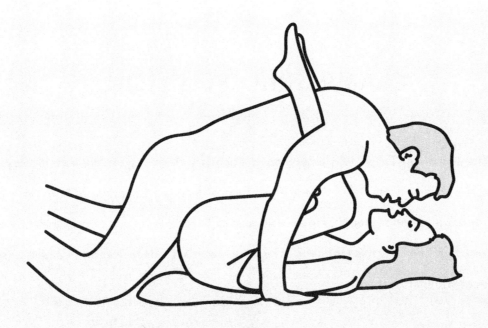

HOUSE NUMBER - POSITION

Time for another hot number! The „House Number" position goes like this: She lies down on the bed and puts a pillow under her bottom. He kneels between her and penetrates her. She encloses his upper body with her legs. He leans forward on his hands and she moves her pelvis up and down.

CLAMP GRIP - POSITION

With the „Clamping Grip" position you get particularly close. It goes like this: He lies on his side, she lies down with her face at his feet, also on the side, next to him. Now she pulls her legs to her breasts. He may have to slide further up or down so that he can penetrate her. She clutches his knees or legs. He has his hands free and can caress her bottom or stimulate her anus.

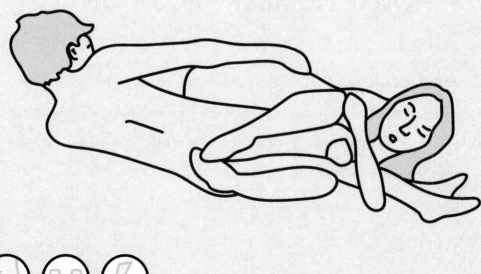

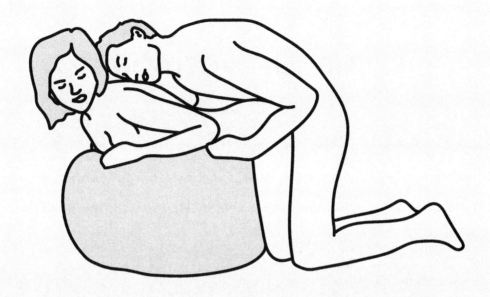

MAGIC MOUNTAINS - POSITION

Try the „Magic Mountains" position today. You need some compact pillows for this.
Stack the pillows on the floor in a small pile of pillows. She kneels in front of the stacked pillows and lets her upper body sink onto the pillows. He kneels behind her and snuggles up to her. She opens her legs slightly so that he can enter her.

THE CLIP - POSITION

Have you ever tried the position „The Clip"? Here's how it works: He lies flat on his back and makes himself comfortable. His legs are closed. She sits on his penis and leans back. She supports herself with her hands. It determines the speed and rhythm of lovemaking.

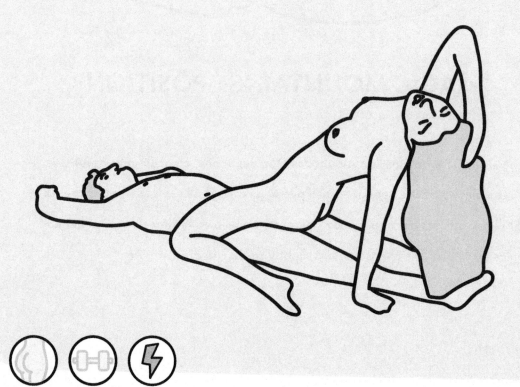

PORTUGUESE GALLEY - POSITION

Set sail with the „Portuguese Galley" position. Here's how it works: He sits on the bed with his legs stretched out and leans back on his hands. She sits down on his lap with her legs bent and her buttocks towards him. She rides him with wavy movements and sets the rhythm.

THE PINBALL - POSITION

A small sporting challenge is the „Pinball" position and it works as follows: He kneels on the floor. She lies down in front of him, also on the floor, with her legs apart. He slides between her legs and lifts her at the waist. She arches her body and he penetrates her. It looks like he's standing at a pinball machine.

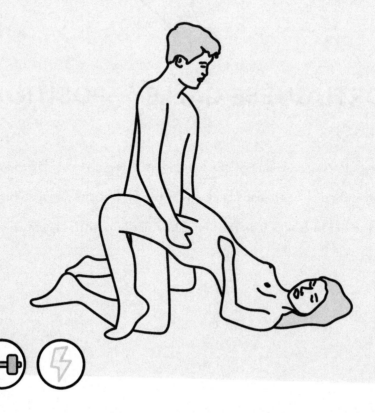

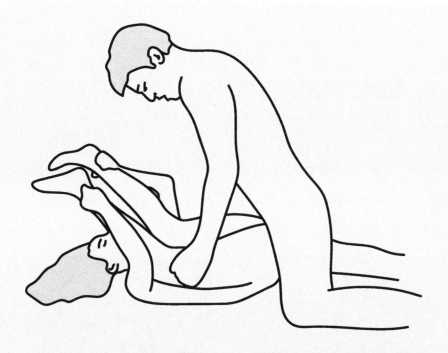

ROCK AND ROLLER - POSITION

Whatever music you prefer, try the „Rock And Roller" position today. Here's how: She lies on the bed and stretches her legs up and then back, like she's doing a roll. He kneels in front of her and opens her legs slightly and holds her waist. He penetrates her while leaning over her body. You can start with a slight rocking motion.

SPLIT BAMBOO - POSITION

It sounds like work, but it definitely isn't. The „Split Bamboo" position goes like this:
She lies flat on her back, spreads her legs, and lifts one leg up. He lies down on her
from the front and penetrates her. She can rest her leg on his shoulder. In this position
he can penetrate her deeply and has his hands free for additional touches.

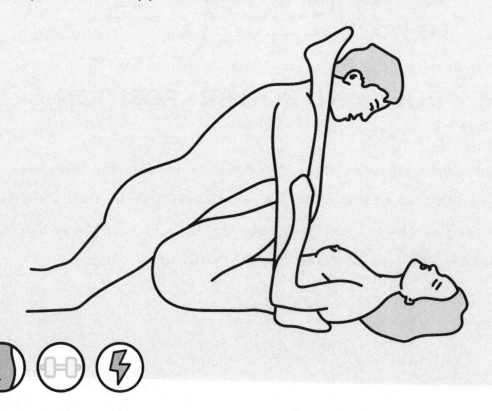

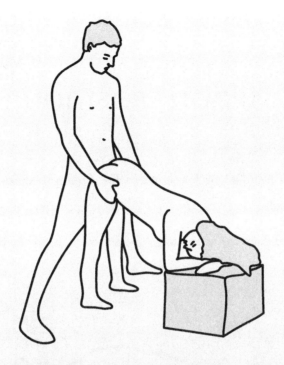

BACK ACT - POSITION

Go and try the „Back Act" position. The position goes like this: She stands with her back to him and spreads her legs slightly. Now she bends forward and can support herself on a piece of furniture, such as a chair, with her forearms. He penetrates her and can stimulate her clitoris with his hands. Also particularly good for anal sex.

SPOON - POSITION

A comfortable position and a popular classic is the „Spoon" position. Both lie sideways on the bed, close to close. She lies in front of him with her back to him so he can penetrate her. This position is particularly good for cuddling. The position is also very suitable for anal sex.

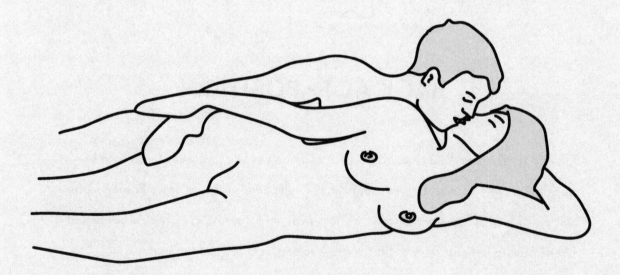

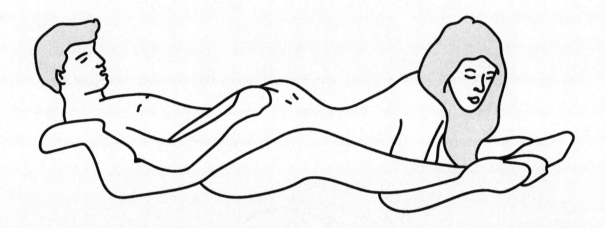

THE BIG X - POSITION

Have you ever tried „The Big X"? This sex position goes like this: He lies flat on the bed with his legs slightly apart. She sits on his penis with her back to him. Now she stretches her legs backwards, her upper body moves forward until she lies flat on him. She can support herself between his feet while she moves slightly up and down.

LOVE PRETZEL - POSITION

Time for the "Love Pretzel" position. This is how it works: Both kneel on the floor opposite each other. He puts his left leg up and she puts her right leg up. Both move close to each other so that he can penetrate her. They hold each other tight and start with slight rocking movements.

FACESITTING - POSITION

Oral sex with a difference: try „Facesitting". One of them lies on the floor and the other sits naked over his or her face. The appeal is the submission and power of love-making. The intensity is determined by the person sitting. She is spoiled by her lying partner with his tongue on the vagina or penis or testicles and bottom.

ANTELOPE - POSITION

How about a new position? If you try the „Antelope" position, this is how it works:
Both stand opposite each other. Now he holds her back with both arms. She climbs
onto his penis and clasps his hips with her legs. A wall can help you keep your balance.
This position is for smaller women and stronger men. If that doesn't work, grab a table
for her to support you.

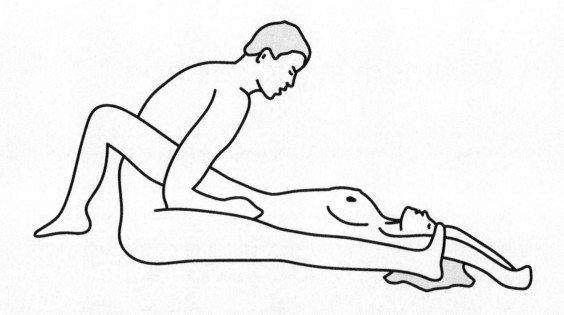

GLOWING JUNIPER - POSITION

Let it glow in bed with the „Glowing Juniper" position. This is how it works: She lies

down on the bed and makes herself comfortable. She spreads her legs slightly and

bends them. He kneels in front of her, between her legs, and lifts her hips onto his lap.

Now he penetrates her and begins the lovemaking with slight rocking movements.

DOGGY STYLE - POSITION

Another classic among the sex positions „Doggy Style". Puts special focus on the doggy style today. She is on all fours as he kneels behind her and penetrates her. A popular position in which the penis penetrates particularly deeply and she enjoys special pleasure from its hard thrusts. He can also smack her on the bottom or lead her by the shoulders or slightly by the hair. For even more intense experiences.

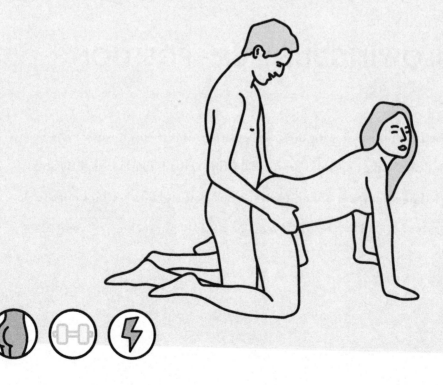

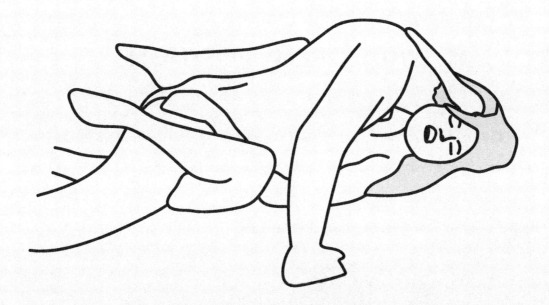

PLAY IT SAFE - POSITION

A safe bet is the „Play It Safe" position and it works like this: She lies on her back and spreads her legs. He lays on top of her and penetrates her while she wraps her legs around him. A romantic position with a lot of body contact, where you can also pamper and caress your partner with your hands.

81

WIDE OPEN - POSITION

Build the „Wide Open" position into your sex play today. The position works like this:
He kneels on the bed. She lies comfortably on her back in front of him, with her head
on a pillow, lifts her bottom and wraps her legs around him. He penetrates her and
supports her with his hands as she arches her back. Good views included.

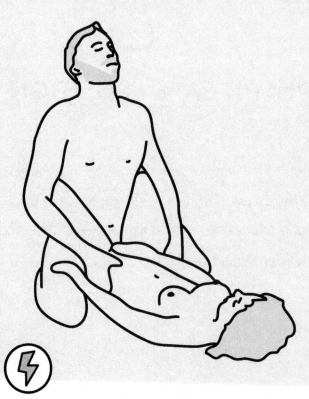

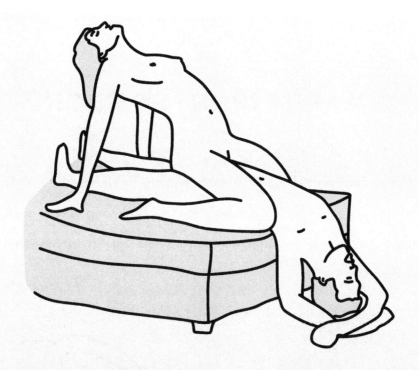

SUPERNOVA - POSITION

Have you ever tried the „Supernova" position? Today is the day! He lies relaxed on the bed with his legs stretched out and his head towards the edge of the bed. She then sits on top of him in a cowgirl position and leans back, propped up on her hands. Now both of them carefully push themselves up until his upper body protrudes backwards over the edge of the bed. His pelvis is still on the bed and his head is comfortably on the floor.

WAFFLE IRON - POSITION

Don't burn your fingers on the „Waffle Iron" position. This is how this position works: He lies comfortably on his back on the bed. She lays flat on top of him, opening her legs slightly so he can enter her. She can control speed and intensity through whole body movements.

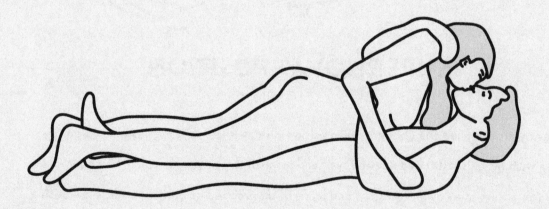

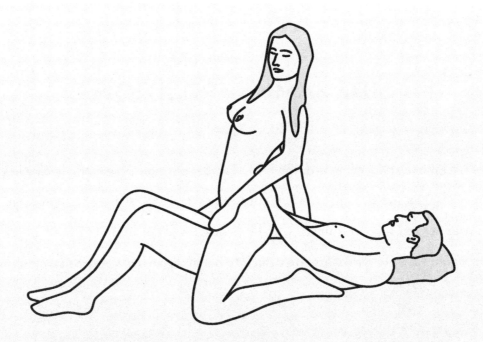

COWGIRL REVERSE - POSITION

Puts a lot of value today on the "Cowgirl Reverse". A popular and well-known position where he lies flat on his back and she sits on top of him like in the cowgirl position. Only with the difference that the butt points in his direction. She determines the rhythm while he can enjoy the sight of her bouncing ass.

SIDE SAMBA - POSITION

There is a bit of dirty dancing with the "Side Samba" position. How to do it: She lies down on the bed and stretches her legs out to the side, in the shape of a right angle. He leans over her and supports himself with his hands. He penetrates her from the side. This position allows him to penetrate deep into her and give her a particularly intense experience.

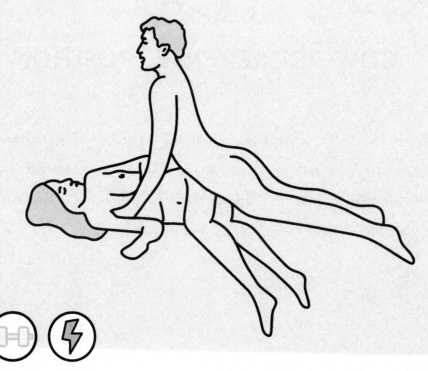

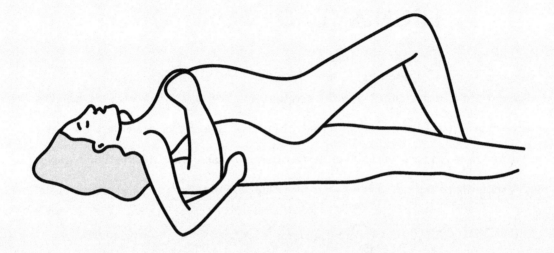

DOUBLE DECKER - POSITION

The „Double Decker" works like this: He lies flat on the bed. She lays her backside flat on him and braces herself with her elbows behind him as he penetrates her. She bends her legs with her feet on his knees. This position is particularly suitable for anal sex.

HIGH AHEAD - POSITION

Today you come to the climax with the position „High Ahead". How it works: She lies comfortably on the bed with a pillow under her head. She stretches her legs up in the air. He kneels in front of her and bends over her. He then penetrates her while moving her legs slightly to the side. He now has free play with his hands to caress her breasts.

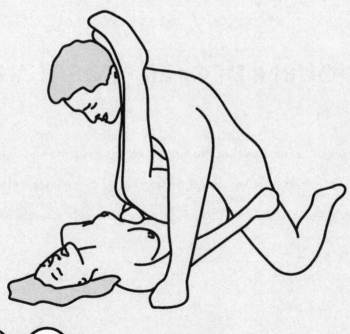

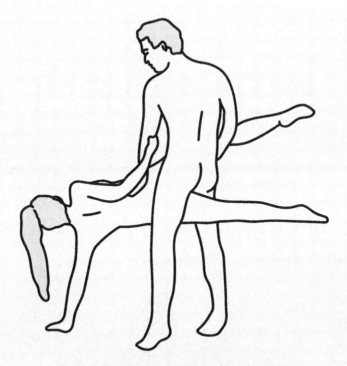

TONGS - POSITION

A sporty position is the „Tongs" position. Here's how she works: She slides off the side of the bed and supports herself with her hand on the floor and her feet on the bed. He steps over her bottom leg and grabs the top leg so the legs lock together. Now he penetrates her and holds her completely without needing the help of the bed any longer.

89

KNEELING - POSITION

Full commitment with the position „Kneeling", it works as follows: Both kneel opposite each other on the bed and hold each other's arms. He pushes his knees and thighs between her legs. She lifts her body up a bit so he can penetrate her. This position allows a lot of physical contact and a particularly romantic experience.

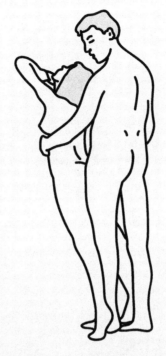

STURDY - POSITION

Try the position the „Sturdy". This is how it works: Both stand up straight and she turns her back on him. His pelvis and her bottom are pressed tightly together as he penetrates her. His hands wrap around her waist and she can lean forward against a wall or a table.

91

THE BIG X REVERSE - POSITION

Try the „Big X Reverse" position. The position works like this: She lies on the bed with her legs slightly apart. He kneels on either side of her hips, buttocks facing her. He then leans forward and penetrates her, stretching his legs back so that he's lying on top of her upside down. For a better grip she can hold on to his legs.

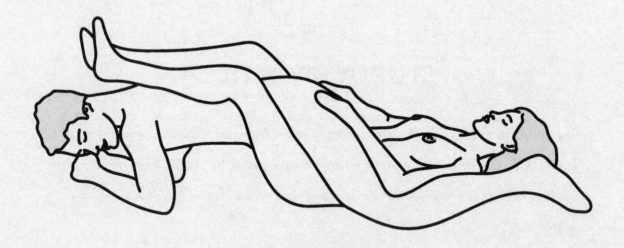

BALANCING ACT - POSITION

Ensures the right work-life-sex balance with the „Balancing Act" position. This is how it works: He lies on his back and pulls his legs towards him. She sits backwards on his penis, he grabs her waist. She can also caress his testicles with her hands.

ELECTRIC CHAIR - POSITION

This electric chair is electric and safe: she stands in front of a chair or couch and leans forward slightly, hands on knees. He is on the chair with his hands on the back and his feet on the edge of the chair/couch. He penetrates her and begins to control the love-making with light movements.

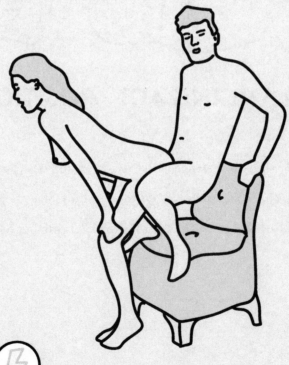

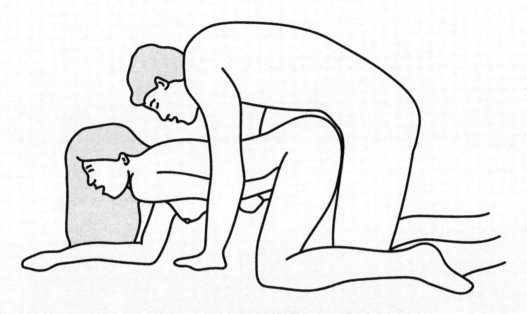

WORSHIP - POSITION

A particularly intense position is the „Worship" sex position. This is how it works: She stands on all fours on the bed. He kneels behind her and enters her from behind. If he now leans his upper body forward, he can massage her breasts with his hands or caress her clitoris. Thus, he can give her special attention and satisfaction.

THE DEVOTION - POSITION

It gets a bit sporty with the „Devotion" position. How it works: She stands in front of the bed and leans on the bed with her legs straight and her elbows all the way down. He stands behind her between her legs and grabs her lower legs. He lifts her, waist level, and penetrates her.

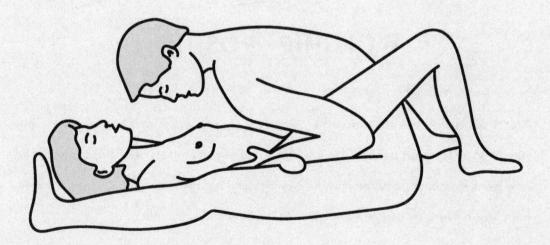

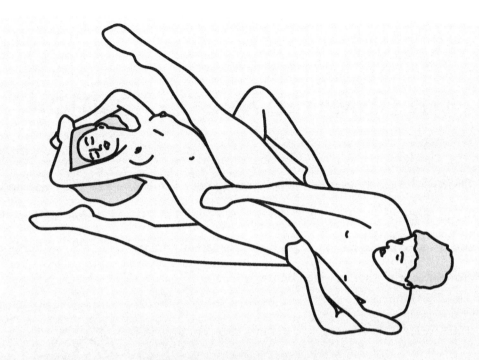

STAR - POSITION

Whether under the starry sky or not, let it glitter with the „Star" position. This is how it works: She lies down on the bed and makes herself comfortable. She puts one leg up and the other is flat. He lies down in front of her with outstretched legs and then slides up to her. One leg is under her flat leg and one leg is between her legs. He slides closer and closer to her until he can penetrate her. After the short „docking manoeuvre" the fun can begin.

THE DISMAYED ANGEL - POSITION

The „Dismayed Angels" position really spices up your sex. Both lie on their side on the bed, in the spoon position, and look in the same direction. He penetrates her from behind and is very close to her. With his hands he can either stroke her all over her body or additionally satisfy her between her legs.

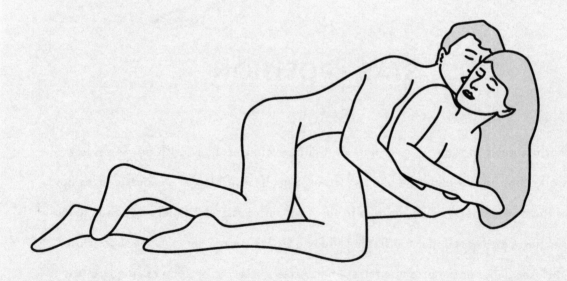

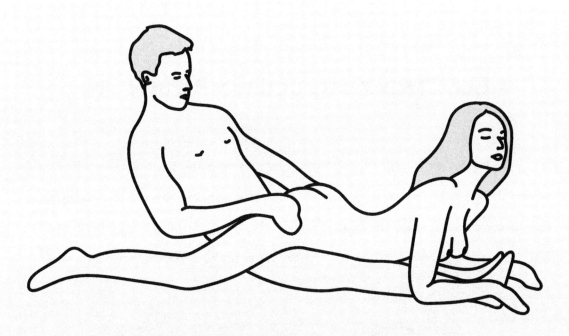

AMAZING VIEW - POSITION

A position with a view is the „Amazing View". Here's how she goes: He sits down on the bed with his legs stretched out. She carefully sits down on his penis with her back to him. Then she stretches her legs backwards and lies forward, with her stomach on his legs, without the penis slipping out. She can support herself with her hands on his feet while he enjoys the view.

ELECTRIFYING SLIDE - POSITION

It's not just good, it's electrifying with the „Electrifying Slide" position. This is how it works: She lies down, legs spread, relaxed on her stomach. He now sits on her thighs so that he can penetrate her. The legs are on her left and right while he supports himself with his hands behind or in front. Now he can move his body forwards and backwards.

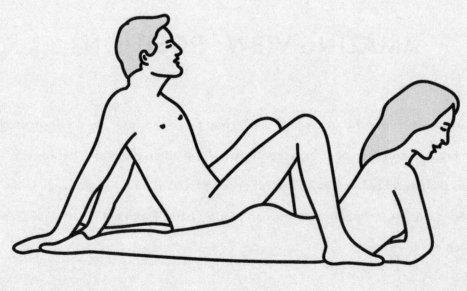

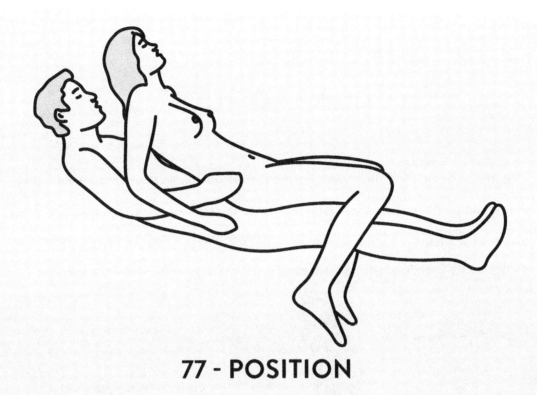

77 - POSITION

The spoon position upgrade is the „77" position. Sex becomes even more intense, especially for women, because the G-spot is specifically stimulated. Lie on your side, He is behind you. Squeeze tightly together, he penetrates her. She now wraps her legs around his, outwards. She bends her legs at 45 degrees, which looks like the number 7, but still stays on it. She now alternates between stretching out her legs or pushing her bottom backwards.

COW - POSITION

It continues beastly with the „Cow" position. While standing, she bends forward until she can support herself on the floor. He then penetrates her while standing. He can then set the rhythm and tempo from behind. With this position, he can penetrate her deeply, which promises her a lot of pleasure. Even if it makes you sweat a lot.

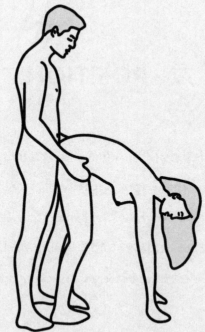

MAHARAJA - POSITION

In this position, she takes the lead. This sensual position is called the „Maharaja"
position. He lies down on the bed or floor and stretches his legs up. She pushes his legs
forward and now sits on his penis with her legs apart. He rests his legs on her shoulder
and enjoys. While she sets the intensity with smooth up and down movements.

We hope you had & have a lot of fun with the 100 positions. If so, give us a rating, we would be happy :)

THANKS ♥

© 2023
Title: 100 sex positions
Author: **Franka Burgmuller**

Looty

Represented by:
web agency
Patricia Theobald and
Yannick Theobald.
Jehle Concept GbR
Hauptstr. 56 – 77756 Hausach

Printed in Great Britain
by Amazon

31701767R00059